HOTEL TRANSYLVANIA
The Series

Mavis
in Charge

Mavis's guide to running a hotel, handling adults, and having fun!

By Delphine Finnegan

KEEP OUT!

Simon Spotlight

New York   London   Toronto   Sydney   New Delhi

SIMON SPOTLIGHT

An imprint of Simon & Schuster Children's Publishing Division
1230 Avenue of the Americas, New York, New York 10020
This Simon Spotlight edition August 2018
TM & © 2018 Sony Pictures Animation Inc. All Rights Reserved.
All rights reserved, including the right of reproduction in whole or in part in any form.
SIMON SPOTLIGHT and colophon are registered trademarks of Simon & Schuster, Inc.
For information about special discounts for bulk purchases, please contact Simon & Schuster Special Sales at 1-866-506-1949 or business@simonandschuster.com.
Designed by Julie Robine
Manufactured in the United States of America 0718 LAK
ISBN 978-1-5344-2200-1
ISBN 978-1-5344-2201-8 (eBook)

CONTENTS

WELCOME TO HOTEL TRANSYLVANIA

Welcome guests!

We are delighted that you have selected the Hotel Transylvania. For more than one thousand years we have happily served you as the premier monster hotel. On behalf of the entire Hotel Transylvania scream team, I extend a very creepy welcome to you and trust your stay with us will be completely uncomfortable, occasionally disgusting, and utterly unforgettable.

The hotel offers a spooky selection of services. Should you require any assistance or have special requirements, please do not hesitate to contact the front desk.

Yours sincerely,
Dracula *Mavis*
Hotel Manager

XOXO

As you enter the lobby, take a moment to stop and enjoy the roasting fire. It's the perfect place to warm bones, thaw gooey insides, and dry off fur. It also makes for a great meet-up location. Not a fan of fire? Try our seating across the lobby—far, FAR away from the flames.

Gift Shop

Our gift shop doors are always open, except when the wolf pups are on the loose. Then we temporarily shut down before they wreck the place. Stop by the gift shop to find the scariest souvenirs and most monstrous memorabilia.

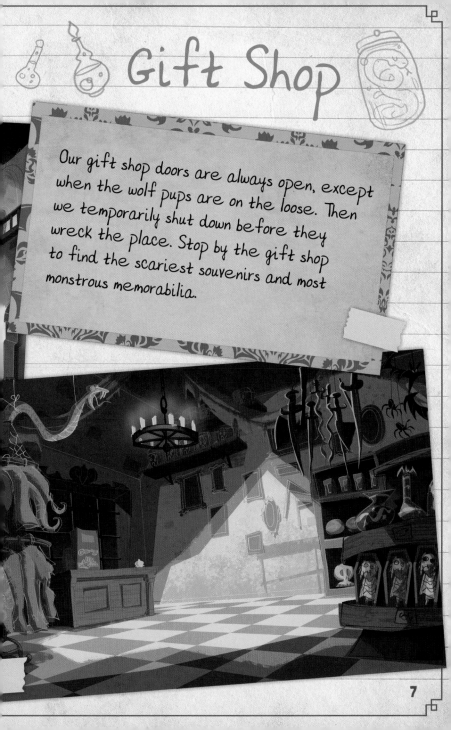

Clubhouse

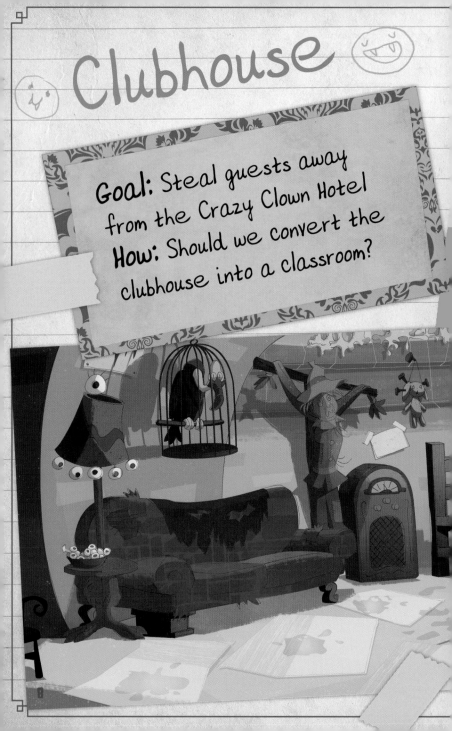

Goal: Steal guests away from the Crazy Clown Hotel
How: Should we convert the clubhouse into a classroom?

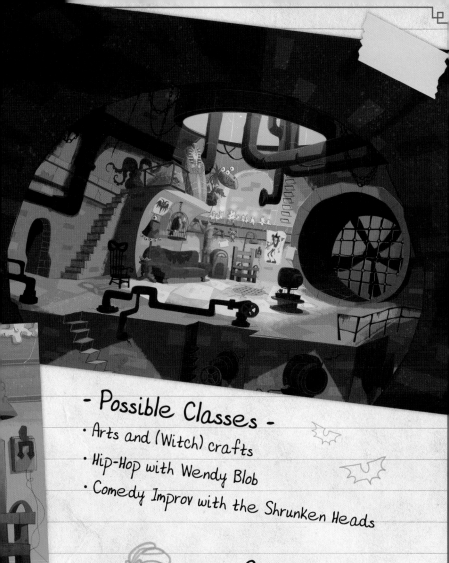

- Possible Classes -

- Arts and (Witch) crafts
- Hip-Hop with Wendy Blob
- Comedy Improv with the Shrunken Heads

Next Steps:

Ask Wendy to—

- Sneak behind enemy lines
- Spy on the Crazy Clown classes
- Report back

Graveyard

In need of a little quiet time? A place to decompress and decompose? Look no further than Hotel Transylvania's graveyard. Be sure to check out the newly buried plots—you never know who you'll find there.

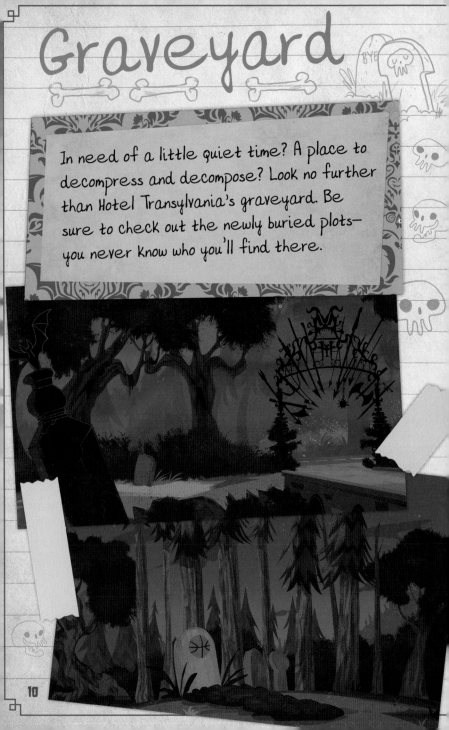

Quasimodo's Kitchen

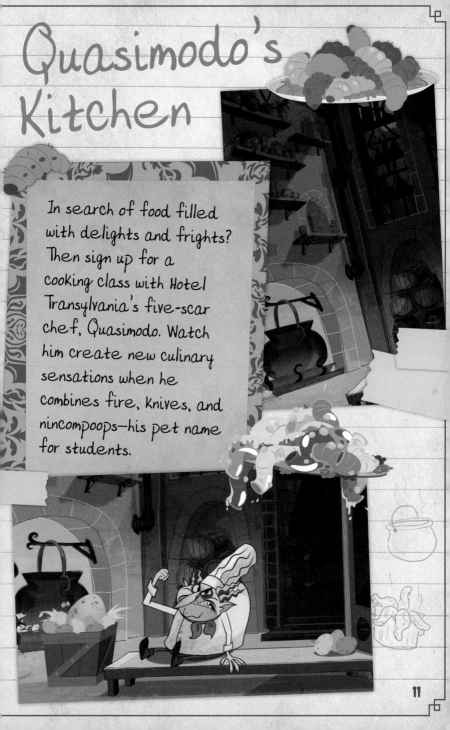

In search of food filled with delights and frights? Then sign up for a cooking class with Hotel Transylvania's five-scar chef, Quasimodo. Watch him create new culinary sensations when he combines fire, knives, and nincompoops—his pet name for students.

Knock-Knocks and Other Jokes
with the Shrunken Head Door Knockers

Knock, knock!

Who's there?

Orange.

Orange who?

Orange you glad you're staying at the Hotel Transylvania?!

What does the Hotel Transylvania turn on during the summer?

The scare conditioner!

Lol

Why is the cemetery a great place to write?

Because there are a lot of good plots there.

MAVIS

Name: Mavis, aka Mavy Wavy, Honey Bat, and a bunch of other Drac-created nicknames

Likes: being in charge of Hotel Transylvania, shaking things up, scream cheese, her friends, her red sneakers

Dislikes: boring old traditions, bossy aunts, cousins who meddle

Guilty pleasure: dreaming about the outside world

Special skills: bat transformation, shaping her shadow, instant outfit changes

Drac
Manager of the world-renowned Hotel Transylvania. Currently on leave while attending the Vampire Council. Devoted father of Mavis.

WENDY

Name: Wendy Blob

Likes: <u>everything</u> but especially being helpful, Jazzercise, and her ponytail

Dislikes: when her dad tries to be the cool dad, getting food stuck in her hair

Guilty pleasure: accidentally on purpose reading diaries

Special skill: breaking into blobettes (they may be much smaller versions of her, but they're as just as enthusiastic)

Bob Blob

Is Wendy's father. His jelly-like body matches his personality. He's easygoing, adaptable to change, and an excellent dancer. Steer clear of him when he's feeling sick. He blows chunks.

19

HANK

Name: Hank N Stein
Likes: hanging out with his friends in their clubhouse, helping Mavis at the hotel, keeping it together ("it" being all his body parts)
Dislikes: fire, matches, anything combustible, spiders, losing his head
Guilty pleasure: being a real boy, but only for a short while
Special skill: herding the wolf pups

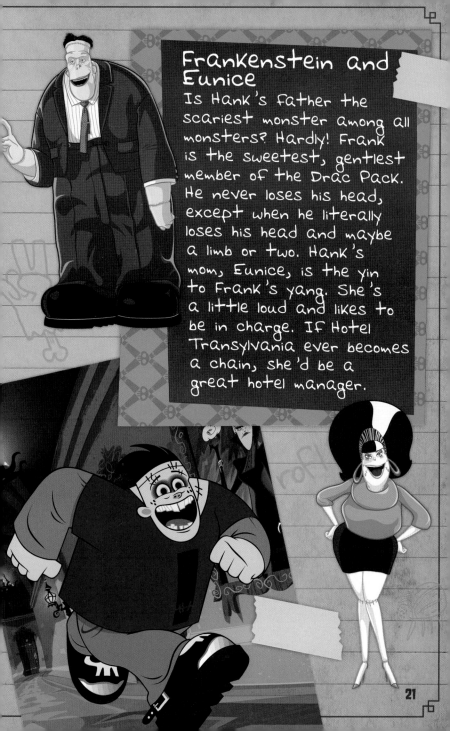

Frankenstein and Eunice

Is Hank's father the scariest monster among all monsters? Hardly! Frank is the sweetest, gentlest member of the Drac Pack. He never loses his head, except when he literally loses his head and maybe a limb or two. Hank's mom, Eunice, is the yin to Frank's yang. She's a little loud and likes to be in charge. If Hotel Transylvania ever becomes a chain, she'd be a great hotel manager.

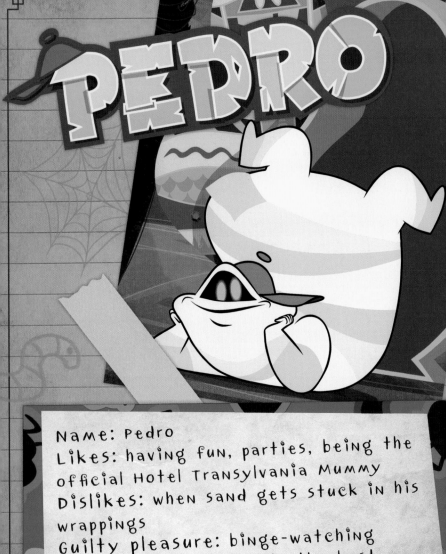

PEDRO

Name: Pedro
Likes: having fun, parties, being the official Hotel Transylvania Mummy
Dislikes: when sand gets stuck in his wrappings
Guilty pleasure: binge-watching *Hotel Pennsylvania*, only the best show on TV
Special skills: breaking through walls, summoning sand storms

Murray

Murray is Pedro's cousin and one of Drac's closest friends. Like Pedro, he loves a good party and will do anything to keep the crowd happy.

Name: Lydia Dracula, aka Aunt Lydia, aka the Dark Baroness

Likes: order, restoring order, tradition, maintaining traditions, logical hotel management, bossing around Diane (her pet chicken)

Dislikes: humans, garlic, disorder, messes, Medusa

Guilty pleasures: the breakfast ghoul-ash served at Hotel Transylvania, rereading Cornelius Shivers novels, her gramophone

Special skill: smelling humans

LYDIA

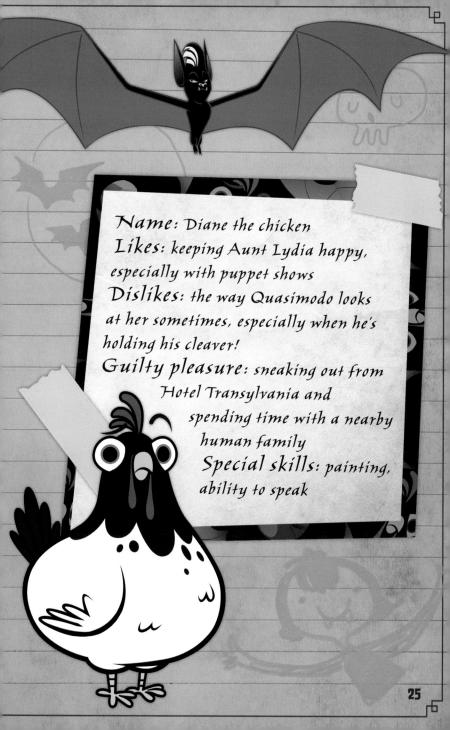

Name: Diane the chicken
Likes: keeping Aunt Lydia happy, especially with puppet shows
Dislikes: the way Quasimodo looks at her sometimes, especially when he's holding his cleaver!
Guilty pleasure: sneaking out from Hotel Transylvania and spending time with a nearby human family
Special skills: painting, ability to speak

Uncle Gene

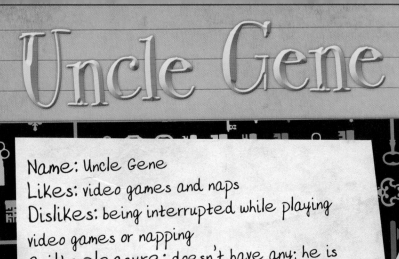

Name: Uncle Gene

Likes: video games and naps

Dislikes: being interrupted while playing video games or napping

Guilty pleasure: doesn't have any; he is incapable of feeling guilty about <u>anything</u>

Special skill: identifying his toe that had been missing for 100 years

KLAUS

Name: Klaus

Likes: phlegm ball, Vamp Offs, victory dances, when his bangs don't get frizzy

Dislikes: losing to his cousin, Mavis; twelfth-century humidity

Guilty pleasure: elaborate plots against Mavis even when they don't work

Special skills: none yet, but he's working on getting the last laugh

QUASIMODO

Name: Chef Quasimodo, aka Quasi

Likes: cooking, baking, expired ingredients with an extra layer of mold

Dislikes: humans, being nice, monsters underfoot in his kitchen, being called Rainbow (his real name)

Guilty pleasure: altering the recipe for breakfast ghoul-ash without telling anyone

Special skills: beating eggs, pounding dough, pinching salt

Cooking with Quasimodo

Whether you're a newbie or practically a sous chef, there's always something to learn from Quasimodo. Select the dish you want to make and get ready to meet the master chef for a cooking lesson you'll never forget.

Hard-Spoiled Eggs

Breakfast Ghoul-ash

Panflakes a la Quasi

Blood Plasma Donuts

Gross-Beef

Worm Sundaes

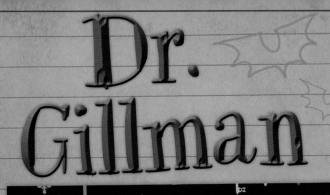

Dr. Gillman

Name: Dr. Gillman

Likes: swimming, sandwiches, winging it, using chain saws in the office

Dislikes: taking tests, following his instincts unless they tell him to ignore Mavis's advice, diagnosing acute cases of exposure to humans

Guilty pleasure: treating the angry corns on Aunt Lydia's feet with salt and butter

Special skill: scare-a-mint gum removal

Dr. Gillman prescribes:

☐ No human contact

☐ Ice packs

☐ Human TV shows
(Important: If it is a repeat of the
Golden Ghouls finale, please, please,
please record for him.)

☐ Sandwiches

MORE Knock-Knocks and Other Jokes
with the Shrunken Head Door Knockers

Knock, knock!

Who's there?

Doris.

Doris who?

Doris locked, that's why I knocked.

Why is Mavis so good at gymnastics?

Because she's an acro-bat!

Why were Pedro's friends annoyed with him?

Because he was wrapped up in himself!

What do you call a haunted chicken?

A poultry-geist.

Why did Diane cross the road?

To get away from
Aunt Lydia.

Why did Diane cross the road?

To visit the humans.

Why did Diane cross the road?

To get away from all these questions!

TOTALLY IN CHARGE

With my dad away, I'm, like, basically in charge.
I know it. My friends know it. The hotel staff
and guests know it. The only person who didn't
know it—or pretended not to—was Aunt Lydia.
So when I heard that Gretchen Squib from
<u>Scream-Cation</u> was coming to review the hotel
today, I knew what to do: spruce up the
hotel, one creaky door at a time, and
impress her so much she'd give the place a
five-skull rating on her blog.
Also, I'd get all the credit.

EEK!

How could I know that instead of fixing a door, I'd let the wolf pups loose, and that they'd knock over Aunt Lydia's statue? Or who could've imagined that in trying to catch the last loose pup with chocolate cake, I'd attract a human into the hotel? Sure things got a little nutty, but Gretchen Squib *loved* the chaos and gave the Hotel Transylvania a great review. Isn't that all that matters?

Order matters. Not breaking works of art matters. —Aunt Lydia

How to Host a Tea Party

Menu: finger sandwiches

Games to play: Hide and Shriek, Hearts

Whom to invite: friends, dolls (ideally dolls who understand the concept of personal space)

Whom <u>not</u> to invite: a Demented Debbie doll. She'll want the tea party to go on forever and will annoy and torment you until the end of time.

Pro tip: If a Demented Debbie doll shows up uninvited, there's only one thing to do: Buy another possessed doll and give it to her! That way she'll never be alone again!

GIVE THE BOY A HAND (OR TWO)

I don't mean to brag, but I'm an amazing gift giver. And I had the greatest gift idea for Hank. There's no getting around it—he isn't any good at basketball. It's a shame because he loves the game.

All it took was one genius idea by moi and a trip to the graveyard where I scored Hank a new set of hands. And not just any hands, but ones that knew how to pass, dribble, shoot, and score! Best gift giver ever? Check!

Except Hank's hands wouldn't let him sleep, eat, or use the bathroom. Dr. Gillman diagnosed a classic case of reverse limb rejection. Hank's old hands faced off against his new, sporty ones. It wasn't pretty to watch, but in the end the old hands won! All in all, it's the thought that counts, right?

41

BUGGING OUT

Work-life balance isn't my strongest skill. It's hard to step away from a twelve-day commitment to a video game filled with exploding giant bugs. But Aunt Lydia's inspection was looming. I raced around the hotel checking everything, right down to testing the guillotine myself. Of course I forgot one item on my to-do list: buy new bedbugs.

Luckily Pedro had a jar of bugs, and we spread them all over the hotel. But they were truth bugs. Soon everyone  was getting mad at each other for telling the truth! Truth bombs were going off everywhere. They weren't the only thing blowing up. The truth bugs could only take so much truth-telling before they imploded. When Aunt Lydia admitted that I belonged at the hotel, I was inspired. I admitted some hard truths, like that I toot in the coffins when no one is around and that I was the one responsible for the truth bug infestation. Kapow! Truth bugs gone.

Good Ideas

- Throw a talent show at the hotel
- Play in a band
- Have fun with friends
- Find Aunt Lydia's long lost friend to distract her
- Ask Uncle Gene for advice

Bad Ideas

- Find Aunt Lydia's long lost friend, Medusa, who is actually her enemy
- Ask Uncle Gene for advice while he's playing a video game
- Try on Medusa's wig
- Turn Medusa into stone*

*Totally worth it because it made Aunt Lydia smile

THAT'S *SO* 12TH CENTURY

Ugh. Klaus. Double Ugh. He's my cousin.
Triple Ugh. He shows up at the worst times,
like in the middle of a phlegm ball game. I was
totally crushing it, like I always do, when poof—
here's Klaus. He's so twelfth century, what with
the fancy suit and fussy hair.
An embarrassment to modern-day vampires.

ugh

Of course he challenged me, and obviously I accepted. I even put up dad's golden fangs as part of the bet. What was I thinking? They're Drac's lucky fangs and a family heirloom! The game got intense and we played all over the hotel for more than three weeks. I'm still not sure the game has ended.

Dr. Gillman's Three-Step Guide to Encountering Humans

1) Admit that humans are the most dangerous creatures on Earth.

2) Avoid combat. You'll be up against their great human strength.

3) In summary: Should you ever encounter a human . . .

Beware. Beware! BEWARE!

Mavis's Guide
to Encountering Humans

1) Wear a human mask.

2) Don't be afraid.

3) Go straight to their door and ring the bell.

4) Commence babysitting.

5) Have fun!

6) Reminder: Humans are nothing to be afraid of.

Reminder: Make humans fear monsters!
—Aunt Lydia

AAAH

CAN A VAMPIRE BLUSH?

Holy rabies! Was I dreaming or did Jett Black, the ridiculously gorgeous teen rock god, check in to Hotel Transylvania? Too bad I totally embarrassed myself with the spider in my teeth! I tried to be low-key the next time I saw Jett. But I didn't realize that I had leeches on my face.

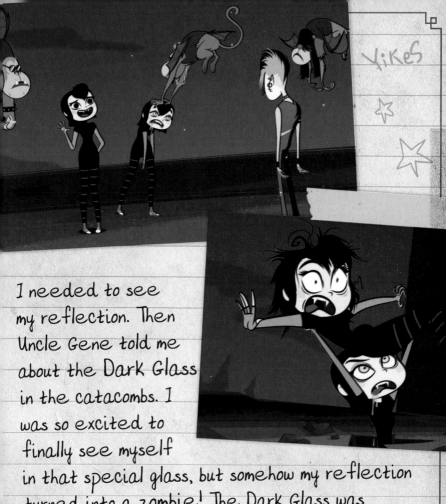

Yikes

I needed to see my reflection. Then Uncle Gene told me about the Dark Glass in the catacombs. I was so excited to finally see myself in that special glass, but somehow my reflection turned into a zombie! The Dark Glass was cursed, something Uncle Gene could have told me earlier! Zombie Mavis tried to stick Jett in the mirror! So humiliating. With Uncle Gene's help, I sent Zombie Mavis back into the mirror. Then I broke it—just in case. One Mavis is more than enough. *I couldn't agree more.*
—Aunt Lydia

HATCHING A PLAN

When it came to my dad's plants, I had one job to do: keeping them alive. And I failed.

Of course I had a brilliant backup plan. What if I got some plants from Quasimodo's garden and swapped them for my dad's dead ones? Wendy and I went to his kitchen. While we didn't get any replacement plants, I took one of Quasimodo's eggs and decided to raise it.

But Quasimodo had other plans. He wanted to cook it. So I had to take my egg, or as I like to call him, Weggsley, everywhere I went, until he hatched! Before long we were playing Creep-a-boo. Soon enough his true nature was revealed. Weggsley wanted to cook me up. Now that's one cracked egg.

TEMPERAMENTAL CHEFS NEED NOT APPLY

Boom-drac-a-lacka! It was just a matter of time before I became employee of the month. I think even Aunt Lydia was impressed. She invited me to join her for Quasimodo's famous breakfast ghoul-ash. When I asked for a smidge of salt, Quasimodo got offended and quit. How would I get him to come back before Aunt Lydia found out? Nothing comes between her and her daily ghoul-ash.

Luckily, Pedro was ready to pitch in. Is there something about that kitchen that turns monsters into bigger monsters? Pedro refused to cook the same meal twice. So I tracked down Quasimodo at a food truck in the hotel driveway. I begged him to come back. Aunt Lydia loved his new, improved ghoul-ash and made him the new employee of the month. Oh well. The crown kept slipping anyway.

THE WAY OF THE BLOB

Never chew gum around Wendy. Never chew gum around Wendy. Never chew gum around Wendy.

If I write it three times, I'll remember it forever, right? I **love** Wendy. She's exactly what you want in a BFF—enthusiastic, adventurous, and rarely says "no" to my genius ideas. And I love her pink ponytail. It totally suits her. She's super protective of it and was so upset when gum got stuck in it. But Dr. Gillman got it out.

Wendy vowed to pay back Dr. G for saving her ponytail by sticking by his side. Sorta extreme. But who am I to question the Way of the Blob? That's what Wendy calls repaying a debt. When she started thanking me and pretty much everyone in the hotel, she ended up creating blobettes—mini versions of herself that stuck by our sides. But all those blobettes were a drain and Wendy's brain started to turn into mush. It's a good thing it's easy to put blobs back together. I'm so glad we restored Wendy to her old self!

BFF♡

Wendy, Wendy, Wendy,
Your blobs are way too trendy,
It's getting loco, very.
You're losing it, it's scary.

Everybody, conga!
Dance-a to this song-a.
The rhythm is so snappy.
It makes the blobbettes happy!

Lol

While the music's playing,
Keep your hips a-swaying.
Hope this works! I'm praying
'Cause Wendy needs some saving!

If you've got a blobette,
Get ready to lob-ette!
That's it, Wendy, bounce high!
Now let's let our blobs fly!
Olé!!

THEIR "LOVE" IS LIKE A DEAD, DEAD ROSE

I am really, really, **REALLY** trying to help Aunt Lydia. She is about to go over the edge and possibly take me with her. It's all because we're hosting the Meeting of the Minds convention. It's the hotel's biggest event and she wants everything to be perfect. But *nothing* is perfect enough for her. No crystal ball can go unpolished. And don't even get me started on how each shrub must look just so. I wish could find something to distract her.

My <u>mission</u>: Get Aunt Lydia off my back.
My <u>accomplice</u>: Wendy, who is also looking to shake her clingy dad.

How to Plan the Perfect Date
115% Guaranteed

- Forge romantic note

- Pick dead flowers

- Pick a time for the date

- Don't tell either party that they're being set up

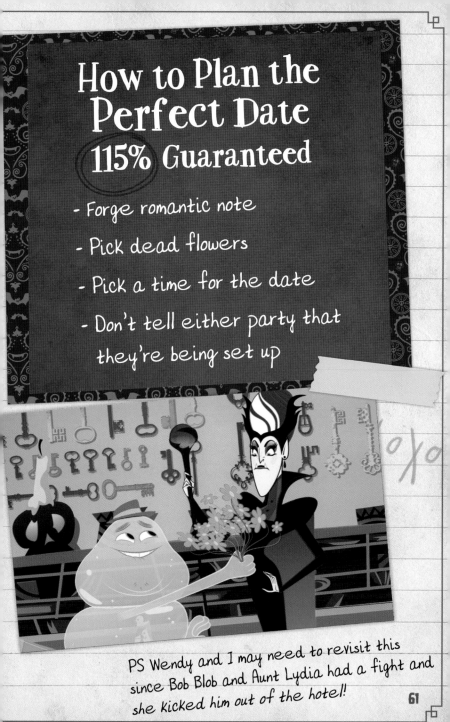

PS Wendy and I may need to revisit this since Bob Blob and Aunt Lydia had a fight and she kicked him out of the hotel!

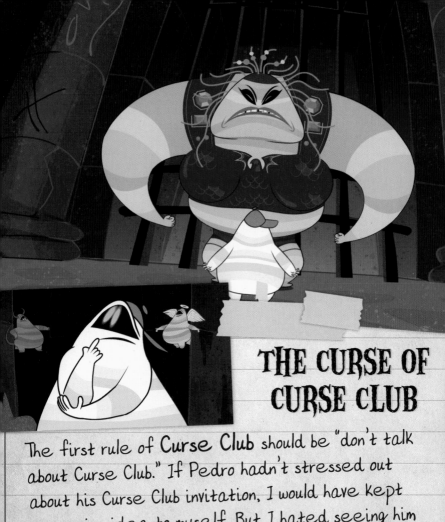

THE CURSE OF CURSE CLUB

The first rule of **Curse Club** should be "don't talk about Curse Club." If Pedro hadn't stressed out about his Curse Club invitation, I would have kept my genius idea to myself. But I hated seeing him so mopey. Pretending his curses worked was pretty brilliant, until it wasn't. I didn't know he'd want to go bandage-to-bandage with another mummy. And not just any mummy, but the legendary Queen Tuttenhammer. How can I make this right? Also . . . how did I end up with a monkey tail?

New Spa Services:
Mummy Curses

All new! The Hotel Transylvania is happy to announce that temporary mummy curses are now available at the spa, provided by our very own Pedro, the master of mummy magic.

Your first curse is complimentary.

Grow hairy toenails

Grow witch warts for eyeballs

Howl like a werewolf

Swap bodies

Turn to mush

Transform ears into carrots

Grow a monkey tail

RUNAWAY CASKET

Total gulp emoji. Diane caught chicken pox. Someone had to watch Aunt Lydia while she rested in her rejuvenation casket, and that someone was me. It was the perfect chance to show her that I am responsible. What could go wrong in one hour or even the one measly minute I stepped away to use the bathroom? Apparently a lot.

Since Dr. Gillman declared the casket contaminated by Diane's pox, the bellhops brought it to the curb, where a <u>human</u> took the casket. Luckily Pedro, Hank, Wendy, and I got the casket back to the castle just in time. Aunt Lydia never knew what happened. *Until now!*
— *Aunt Lydia*

Things I'd rather do than watch
Aunt Lydia sleeping in her casket:

Witness Pedro unraveling

Wax the hair off yeti backs at the spa

Have a tea party with my Demented
Debbie doll

Listen to Klaus's trash talk

ugh

WHAT HAPPENS IN ROOM 1313 . . .

I'd **sooo** rather be at the party in room 1313. Those flies know how to throw a great bash. But it's safer to do what Aunt Lydia wants, like pre-slime the hotel room keys. On the plus side, if I hadn't been at the front desk, I wouldn't have seen Aunt Lydia lose it when her favorite author, the cockroach Cornelius Shivers, checked in. She was giddy and giggling. Could she have been possessed?

Of course Cornelius had to stay in room 1313. Luckily, I got a message up to the room and somehow they cleaned up the party before we walked through the door. Phew! Room 1313 was so well cleaned that they even got rid of the ghost who lived in there. Great, right? Wrong!

That ghost happened to be the ghost writer behind *all* of Cornelius's books. Without her, he would never turn in his next book. And if Aunt Lydia found out we were the cause of Cornelius's writer's block, her giggling would be replaced with a scowl.

I get why the ghost did not want to return. Freedom feels and tastes so good. So instead Hank, Pedro, Wendy, and I wrote the entire book for Cornelius in one night. It's a *little* rough around the edges. I wonder if anyone will notice.

THIS IS HANK

He's a monster full of stitches and afraid of fire. Sometimes he misplaces body parts. And if I'm being honest, sometimes we take the parts without asking. I know, I know. Not cool. But his big feet are perfect for making noise in tap dance class. Just ask Wendy. He never seemed to mind until recently.

AND THIS IS HANK

My brilliant idea to make his parts less removable didn't go as planned. I'm not exactly sure how it happened. Lightning plus a lot of office supplies is a very powerful combination. Not a stitch in sight and all one piece. And what's with the pale skin and light hair? Hank is . . . a human. If we don't reverse his condition soon, he'll start eating bacon and wearing sweatpants like real humans! I should probably check the forecast. Hopefully lightning will strike twice.

Staff Notice #161632

To properly dispose of stinky mummy wraps, please implement the following steps:

- Collect wraps in a pile
- Beat with an ax
- Set on fire (Hydra available to help)
- Toss remaining ashes off a cliff

Staff Notice #161633
EFFECTIVE IMMEDIATELY
This notice replaces
Staff Notice #161632

Do not discard any guest's mummy wraps, even those that smell like barf.
Wraps are made from an extremely rare polyfester-rotton blend. Any attempt to substitute this material may result in a change of personality and, in rare cases, a mummy may be reduced to a pile of sand. Please adopt these new steps:

- Wash wraps with great care

- Let wraps drip dry

- Do not stand downwind of drying wraps

Get Your *Vamp Off* On

Want to learn about a terrifying, ancient vampire custom? Then join us in the hotel gym every Wednesday at midnight for a lively discussion of Vamp Offs!

Discover how vampires learn to:

- Look angry
- Stare down opponents
- Speak through gritted teeth
- Change and hold poses

Following the discussion there will be a demonstration of poses like Rabid Marauding Minotaur, Juggling Clown Circus, Zombie Mermaid, and Dying Swamp Creature.*

*Management requests that any vampire guests joining the demonstration wear fang guards.

ROCK 'N' ROT

Nothing comes between me and my chance to see Jett Black at Roachella. Not even out-of-touch, pop-music-hating Aunt Lydia. Technically she said "no" and actually took my tickets. **Ugh!** She's too

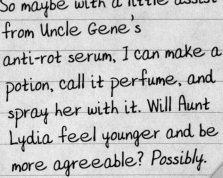

old and can't relate to me. So maybe with a little assist from Uncle Gene's anti-rot serum, I can make a potion, call it perfume, and spray her with it. Will Aunt Lydia feel younger and be more agreeable? Possibly.

There are moments in your afterlife that you remember forever. This night.
This concert.
This song is one of those moments.
Jett Black sang a song that I wrote!!

Slug Guts
by Mavis Dracula

Slug guts in my
hairrrrrrrrrr.
Slug guts
everywherrrrrrrrrre.
AND I DON'T REALLY
CARRRRRRRRRRRE!

Warning: This song may reverse the effects
of anti-rot serum. If side effects occur, limit
exposure to pop music immediately.

UNRAVELED

Pedro was stressing out about something. Who would've thunk it? Sure, a visit from his mummy mommy was important, but this was something more. Then Pedro came clean. He'd been telling his mother that he ran Hotel Transylvania. I knew a thing or two about living up to a parent's high expectations. Could we pretend he ran the place? Drac-solutely!

Luckily, Aunt Lydia was reading the newest Cornelius Shivers book. As long as the book kept her occupied, the plan would work.

No such luck.
Aunt Lydia showed up,
insulted Pedro, and
before anyone knew it,
she'd been frozen by
her own spell. Pedro's
relief turned into
something much more—
he started to believe
he was in charge. He
had everyone treat him like royalty.

ugh

After sending almost everyone to the dungeon and risking total destruction of the hotel, Pedro confessed everything to his still-proud mummy mommy. One again, I could totally relate to the proud parent moment.

WITH A WAVE OF A WAND

Aunt Lydia wanted a birthday party for Diane, and I was more than up for the challenge. Talk about a tough crowd! Still, it was a night they'll never forget . . . even if I wanted them to!

WELCOME TO
DIANE:
A NIGHT OF CELEBRATION

With your host, Pedro

Refreshments include: scare-it cake with scream-cheese frosting

HEADLINE ENTERTAINMENT BY MAGICIAN OCTAVIO THE AWESOME

Note to self: When a magician runs away due to fear of Aunt Lydia, do not, and I repeat, DO NOT, use his magic wand without testing it first.

PS Avoid spells that make the guest of honor disappear.

PPS Be ready to track your missing guest of honor into another strange realm.

PPPS Pretend this was your plan all along.

THE VERY, VERY BAD SEED

So we might have been spying on Quasimodo today. And maybe we saw that he was mistakenly given garlic seeds. And it's possible that we opened them up, so I could prove that garlic isn't bad for vampires. It's not. No big deal.

How was I to know that leaving behind one small seed and it would grow into a bulb Aunt Lydia would find, which would make her shut down the hotel for garlic decontamination?

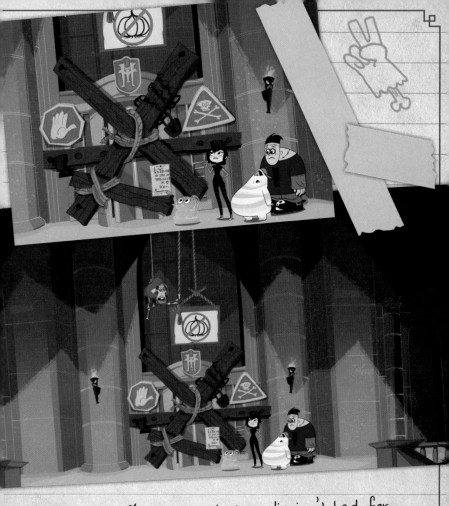

I'm still 110% certain that garlic isn't bad for
vampires. But as the daughter of Dracula, I
know what the optics would be like if anyone
found out I was responsible for dropping the
garlic seeds. Dad would be so disappointed I
teamed up with Quasimodo to find the garlic.
The things I do for family!

WHAT'S IN A NAME?

When the name is Mavy Wavy and my dad (and <u>only</u> my dad) is saying it, then it's a sweet nickname. Silly? Yes. A little embarrassing? That, too. But when said dad signed an endorsement deal and used my nickname for the product name—that was sort of cool. He thought the Mavy Wavys were the height of batwing fashion.

Too bad the Mary Warys didn't _exactly_ work. I broke dishes, spilled shakes, and stumbled through every doorway in the hotel. Talk about a winged nightmare! Tossing them out the window? Best feeling <u>ever</u>. Except those goofy wings couldn't just float off into the sunrise. Nuh-uh. That would be too easy for me. Instead, they glided their way into a human's yard.

yikes

Why did everyone in the castle assume that the humans broke into the castle and stole the Mavy Wavys? Was it really so serious that Dad had to call in using the Vampire Council's emergency crystal ball? And if Aunt Lydia had her way, a monster attack on the humans was the only solution!

One awkward, failed mission to get the wings back was enough. I knew what I had to do.

I came clean with Dad. I hated disappointing him. He wasn't too upset. Because Drac is actually the coolest monster ever. Aunt Lydia, on the other hand—she was not cool about anything.

Drac really is the best dad, even when he makes dorky decisions about products, like the Mary Savey, which should make pool safety cool.

This one . . . I may not wear around the hotel. But it's a definite keeper.

I still think a show of force is not out of the question. —Aunt Lydia

SHE'S BA-ACK!

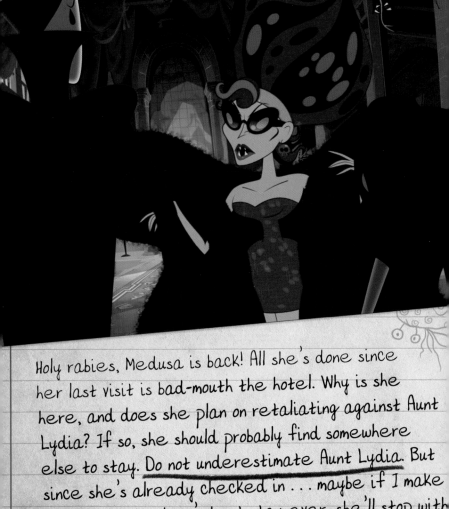

Holy rabies, Medusa is back! All she's done since her last visit is bad-mouth the hotel. Why is she here, and does she plan on retaliating against Aunt Lydia? If so, she should probably find somewhere else to stay. Do not underestimate Aunt Lydia. But since she's already checked in . . . maybe if I make sure this is Medusa's best stay ever, she'll stop with the TV interviews.

Thank you, dear girl.
—Aunt Lydia

Hmmm. Once I saw Aunt Lydia's changing hairstyles, I wasn't all that interested in making sure Medusa enjoyed herself. There was only one likely suspect behind Aunt Lydia's hair situation. I was ready to face Medusa and her snakes—with some stone-proof sunglasses on.

SO CLOSE AND YET SO FAR

Or should I say "so *Klaus* and yet so far"?

It really felt like Aunt Lydia was warming up to me recently. But then Klaus returned and they were closer than ever.

I knew what to do. I snuck into Aunt Lydia's room and polished her casket till it gleamed. While I was at it, I polished her gramophone. And while I was at that, I scratched a beat or two for Pedro.

But then Klaus startled me, and I broke the needle on Aunt Lydia's gramophone. He saw the whole thing. Of course he held it over my head.

With Klaus there's always a way out. I just needed to figure out what he wanted. And what he wanted was bat transformation lessons. So I showed him how to transform and it worked! Win-win.

Plus, he took the blame for the broken needle. Someday I might earn Aunt Lydia's respect. For now, I'm just glad I don't have to listen to that one song she plays over and over and over again.

EVEN MORE Knock-Knocks and Other Jokes
with the Shrunken Head Door Knockers
This is the last of it. We promise.

Knock, knock!

Who's there?

Dewey.

Dewey who?

Dewey have to keep telling silly jokes?

Why did Aunt Lydia get thrown out of the hotel?

Because she was a pain in the neck.

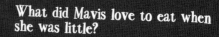

What did Mavis love to eat when she was little?

Alpha-bat soup.

PLEASE TAKE A MOMENT

Thank you for choosing the Hotel Transylvania. We hope that your stay here was exactly as promised. We continue to make *foul yet modern* changes to the hotel. Your feedback is important and appreciated! Please take a moment to fill out this survey.

Please answer the following questions using the scale below— with "1" being the worst and "5" being the best.

scale: **1** = icky **2** = gross **3** = disgusting **4** = vile **5** = revolting

1) Overall condition of the hotel:

    1   2   3   4   5

2) General condition of your guest room:

    1   2   3   4   5

3) Lumpiness of mattress and pillow:

    1   2   3   4   5

4) Fungus level in bathroom:

    1   2   3   4   5

5) Quality of food:

    1   2   3   4   5

Additional comments:

foul yet *modern* changes to the hotel. Your ~~~
and appreciated! Please take a moment to fill out this survey.

Please answer the following questions using the scale below—
with "1" being the worst and "5" being the best.

scale: 1 = icky   2 = gross   3 = disgusting   4 = vile   5 = revolting

1) Overall condition of the hotel:
1   2   3   4   ⑤

2) General condition of your guest room:
1   2   3   ④   5

3) Lumpiness of mattress and pillow:
1   2   3   4   ⑤

4) Fungus level in bathroom:
1   2   3   4   ⑤

5) Quality of food:
1   2   3   4   ⑤

Additional comments:

While I loved the fighting and general chaos caused
by the truth bugs, I still get sentimental about my
previous bedbugs experiences here. Otherwise #2
would be a 5!

DEST BAD FRIDAY EVER! I'VE ALREADY MADE A
RESERVATION FOR NEXT CENTURY'S BAD FRIDAY. KEEP UP
THE GOOD WORK.

The appearance of a human child in the hallways was just the
unexpected surprise I've come to expect from Hotel
Transylvania. Thanks for the scare!

Mavis, I knew I smelled a human!
—Aunt Lydia

Dear Mavis,

My loveable Little Poison Berry, I miss you more than you can possibly imagine. But I am certain you are doing a wonderful job keeping the hotel running smoothly—at least, most of the time. I knew this in my heart, long before your aunt Lydia mentioned that you've been keeping a journal. Yes, my Honey Bat, your aunt takes a peek at it from time to time. Please know that my sister means well. She is bound by tradition and feels a sense of family honor, especially while I attend the Vampire Council. Yes, she may see your journal as evidence of chronic goof-ups. But I know that when you look back on your writing, it will only help you spread your wings and grow. It is not easy to run Hotel Transylvania. Trust me, I know. I can tell you are learning and growing. You make me proud, my Mavy Wavy. So keep writing and planning. Make time for your friends. And don't forget to keep the humans out.

    Love,

    Dad

PS It might be best, Coffin Cake, to stay out of your aunt's room. Her attachment to her gramophone and that song defies explanation. Some questions are better left unanswered.